Aberdeenshire Libraries
www.aberdeenshire.gov.uk/libraries
Renewals
Downl
www.aberdeensh

KT-429-093

ABERDEENSHIRE LIBRARIES

1915785

THE
GRIM GHOST

Illustrated by Helen Flook

A & C Black • London

JF

First published 2008 by
A & C Black Publishers Ltd
38 Soho Square, London, W1D 3HB

www.acblack.com

Text copyright © 2008 Terry Deary
Illustrations copyright © 2008 Helen Flook

The rights of Terry Deary and Helen Flook to be identified as the
author and illustrator of this work have been asserted by them in
accordance with the Copyrights, Designs and Patents Act 1988.

ISBN 978-0-7136-8961-7

A CIP catalogue for this book is available from the British Library.

All rights reserved. No part of this publication may be reproduced
in any form or by any means – graphic, electronic or mechanical,
including photocopying, recording, taping or information storage
and retrieval systems – without the prior permission in
writing of the publishers.

This book is produced using paper that is made from wood grown in
managed, sustainable forests. It is natural, renewable and recyclable.
The logging and manufacturing processes conform to the
environmental regulations of the country of origin.

Printed and bound in Great Britain by
CPI Cox & Wyman, Reading, RG1 8EX

ONE

Rome, AD 113

"Pass me the parrot, Pertinax!"
Augusta shouted across the kitchen.

Augusta's grandson picked up
the large red-and-yellow bird
and carried it across to the bench,
where she was chopping herbs.

The kitchen stoves were burning
and the slaves were sweating.
Pertinax was a skinny boy, and
struggled to carry the dead bird.

"Here it is, Grandma. What are you going to do with it?"

"Chop off the head," said Augusta.

"What for, Grandma?"

"Because my master, Pliny, wants to eat the head," she explained, neatly chopping it off. "Now, pluck out the feathers, and we'll eat the rest for dinner."

"Why would you want to eat a parrot's head?" Pertinax asked.

Before Augusta could answer, the kitchen door swung open and a tall man in a toga stood there.

His narrow face and eagle nose made him look a little like a parrot himself.

Augusta and all the slaves
bowed low. The cook grabbed
her grandson's neck and forced
him to bow, too.

"Master Pliny,"
she cried. "What
an honour to
see you in my
humble kitchen.
What can I get
for you? The wild
boar is roasted,
ready for tonight.
I'm sure I could
carve you a slice
with some tasty
garum sauce..."

"No, no," the master said, with a
wave of the hand. "I am far too

worried to eat a thing. This is the largest feast I have ever held. Some of the greatest men in Rome will be here tonight. If the food and wine is poor, I will die of shame."

Augusta gave a fat grin. "It will all be fine, sir. I've even brought my grandson, Pertinax, here to help."

"Ah, good, good," Pliny muttered. "Excuse me... it's so hot in here, I feel faint."

"Step into the garden, sir, and I'll bring a cup of ale to cool you," said the cook.

The kitchen door was already open, but there was no cooling breeze inside. Pliny moved out and sat on a bench in the shade of a tree.

Augusta took a silver goblet, stepped into the dark, chilly larder and dipped it into a barrel of cool ale. She carried it into the garden. Pertinax followed.

TWO

"There you go, master," the cook smiled. "Stop worrying. Remember, when I was a girl I helped cook for the Emperor Vitellius. What a man! What an eater! We made banquets like yours three or four times every day. That man was a glutton. He lived for food."

Pliny sipped at the ale and nodded. "I have heard the stories about him. He died when I was just six years old, so I never met him. But he was famous for his eating."

"Famous and foul," said Augusta. "It was murder cooking for him, I can tell you."

"Why, Grandma?" Pertinax asked.

"Because it was a waste."

"Didn't he like your food?"

"He liked it *too* much," Augusta sighed.

Pliny nodded. "They say he would eat and eat till his stomach was full. Then he would take a large bowl and push a long feather into his mouth. He'd tickle the back of his throat till he threw the food back up. When his stomach was empty, he'd start eating all over again."

"What a wicked waste," Augusta moaned. "The slaves would have enjoyed that food. Or the poor people of Rome."

Pliny snorted. "Of course it wasn't just the poor people who hated his habits. He used the Roman navy to sail the world and find him new treats. At one feast, they say he had 2,000 fish and 7,000 birds."

"Parrots?" Pertinax asked.

"Probably," Pliny nodded. "I wasn't there."

"But *I* was," Augusta reminded him. "Vitellius was very fond of the rarest foods, like pike livers, pheasant brains and flamingo tongues.

"In the end, the Roman people became tired of his silly ways – they sent an army to kill him.

"Vitellius tried to hide in a cupboard at the temple. They dragged him out, hacked him to death and threw his body into the River Tiber."

Pliny chuckled. "His fat corpse must have made a fine feast for the fish. The pike had their revenge. Ha!"

THREE

Pertinax looked at the parrots on the table, and then up at Master Pliny. "My grandma says you want to eat the parrot heads," he said, shyly. "Why?"

"Sorry, sir," Augusta said. "The boy doesn't understand. Food has to *look* exciting as well as taste delicious. It has to look so exciting that the guests *talk* about it. Parrot heads add a lot of colour to a feast. Now, excuse me, sir, we should get back to the kitchen."

"Leave the boy here for a while," her master said. "He is good company."

Augusta bowed and went back into the scorching kitchen.

"But you can't *eat* parrot heads," Pertinax argued. "You can't chew the feathers – and the beak would break your teeth!"

Pliny sipped his ale and smiled. "The guests use a small spoon to scoop out the boiled brains and eat them."

"Is that why we have so many birds in cages in the kitchen? Will they all have their brains eaten?" Pertinax asked.

"No," Pliny said. "Remember what your grandmother said about exciting food? Well, when the wild boar has cooled, we'll pop a dozen birds inside the empty boar and stitch it up. When the slaves carve open the boar at the feast, the birds will fly out!"

"Old fat-guts Vitellius would have enjoyed that," the boy said.

"I'm sure he'll be there tonight," Pliny murmured.

"But he's dead!"

"His spirit still lives on. When we die, our spirit remains, you know."

Pertinax shivered. "Ghosts? I've heard of them. But they join the gods on their mountain, don't they?"

Pliny blew out his cheeks. "Not all of them. Some stay behind and are doomed to haunt this earth. In fact there was one in this very garden..."

Pertinax gasped. "Have you seen it? Have you seen the ghost, Master Pliny?"

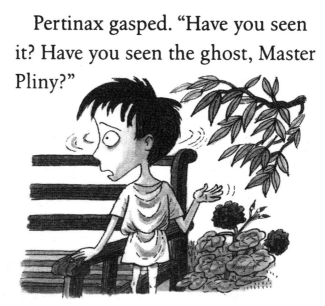

Pliny sipped his ale and looked around the garden. "I cannot tell you," he said slowly. "I would be mocked. I am an important man."

"Grandma says you are a friend of the emperor," the boy nodded.

"I am. So we cannot have people saying Pliny is a foolish man who thinks he sees ghosts."

Pertinax nodded. "I can see that. Maybe... maybe you could tell it as if it happened to someone else? Somewhere else?"

Pliny half-closed his eyes and thought. "I could. Let's say this story happened in Greece... in Athens."

"In a garden that looked like this?" Pertinax grinned.

"In a garden like this. A lot like this..."

Then Pliny told his story.

And this is what he said...

FOUR

The house in Athens was beautiful. It was large and cool, and the garden was full of colours and shades, flowers and sighing trees. The family that lived there had been so very happy.

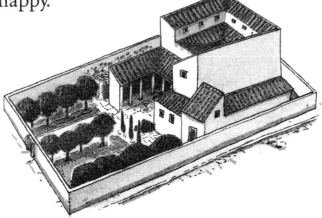

Then, one night, a storm brewed and bubbled in the purple skies over Athens. A flash of lightning lit the rooms, and the crash of thunder woke the heaviest sleepers.

The thunder rumbled out over the ocean and left a soft silence that comes before the rain. And in that silence, the family heard sounds. Sounds like the rattling of chains.

At first, the rattling seemed far away. But with each moment it grew nearer and nearer until it deafened everyone. They all rushed to the great dining room, and huddled together in fear.

The slaves clutched each other in the dark corners of the room. Some tried to scream, but no sound came from their throats.

There was a silver flash of lightning and everyone waited, breathless, for the thunder. When it came, it sounded like the mighty clash of a thousand chains.
A freezing wind blew open the shutters and they turned to look at the light glowing at the window.

The light seemed to shift and change and take on the shape of a man.

No one could breathe. The
glowing man looked ancient. He had
a flowing, white beard and long,
grey hair that streamed in the wind.

His hands and chains rattled and
clattered. He opened his mouth as if
to speak... or scream. But no sound
came. His eyes glowed like great
Moon-green globes. His face showed
terror. As he stepped into the room,
there was a final clash of thunder
and chains, then he vanished.

The rains came. They fell on the empty garden, smashed onto the roof tiles and gurgled in the gutters.

The shaken family and slaves clung to one another as they went back to their beds. But one old slave didn't move anywhere. The ancient cook was stiff and still and staring. She had died of fright.

Morning came after a dreadful night of storms. Yet the grim ghost of the spirit seemed to hang on. No one could see the old man in the daytime... but everyone could feel him watching.

The second night was not as bad as the night before, but the faint rattle of chains let no one sleep.

The next morning, the master of the house gathered together the tired family and slaves. "We are selling the house," he said. "We are moving away from this place that the gods have cursed."

Before the day was over, the house was empty and became the lair of the grim, grey ghost.

FIVE

No one wanted to live there.
The house was cheap, a gift, but
the spirit was too fearsome
for most families to face.

Then, one day,
Dorus the teacher
came to the city
looking for
somewhere to live.
He asked many
questions, and the
master of the house
told Dorus the terrifying truth.

"Even in the daytime the spirit will drive you mad with fear," he warned.

Dorus nodded. "I know the sort of monster you mean. It sounds unhappy."

"Unhappy! Not so unhappy as the slave woman it scared to death. Good sir, we would like to sell the house – of course – but are you sure you want it?"

"I'm sure," Dorus nodded. He decided to buy the place and no one could talk him out of it.

A few days later, Dorus moved in. He had a special seat put at the window. First he ordered his writing tablet and pen...

Then he ordered torches to
be lit...

Finally, he did a strange and brave
thing... he sent all the slaves away
so that he was alone in the house
with the haunted garden.

Night fell. Dorus waited...

In Pliny's garden, the old man sipped the last of his ale.

"And then?" Pertinax breathed. "Then?"

"Did the ghost attack him?"

Pliny gave a secret smile. "I can't remember," he murmured.

"Can't remember!" the boy cried. "Why not?"

Pliny shrugged. "Because my cup of ale is empty. I think I need another one."

Pertinax groaned, but took the cup and ran into the scorching kitchen to fill it up.

A slave girl was stuffing dormice with sausage to roast in the oven.

Another was pulling snails from a bowl of red stuff to boil them.

"What's that?" Pertinax asked.

"Blood," the girl told him. "Snails taste better if you let them feed in a dish of blood for a few days."

Pertinax hurried over to the larder and filled up the cup with ale. He wondered if there would be more blood in Pliny's ghostly tale...

SIX

Pertinax dashed back into the
garden and handed the cool ale to
Pliny. The man supped it and said,
"Look at the birds in the trees."

"Birds? You were telling me about ghosts," Pertinax groaned.

"The birds have no spirits – there are no ghost birds to haunt us. If there were, we would never sleep. We catch them, kill them and eat them. Imagine if their sprits wanted revenge!"

"Is that what the ghost in Dorus's house wanted?" the boy asked. He wanted Pliny to get back to the story.

"No. The ghost wanted peace, not revenge," Pliny replied and went on with his tale...

That first night, Dorus sat at his seat by the window. He went on with his writing. "If you have an empty mind, devils rush in to fill it," the teacher said to the empty room.

It was quiet and calm in the garden. But at the darkest hour, Dorus heard the faint rattle of chains.

The noise grew louder, closer, but still the teacher went on with his writing and ignored the sounds that were in the house and in the room.

At last, Dorus put down his pen and looked up. The ghost was there – the old man with the white beard and flowing hair.

The spirit made a sign for Dorus to come to it. Dorus picked up his pen and went on writing.

The ghost grew angry. Soon
the chains were rattling over the
teacher's head. Dorus looked up
and saw the figure signal for him
to follow.

He picked up a torch and watched as the ghost wandered out into the garden. Dorus followed.

When the grey-haired spirit reached the middle of the garden, it faded and disappeared. Dorus placed a torch on the spot where it vanished. He went back inside the house, yawned and stretched. He decided it was time to get some sleep. Tomorrow would be a busy day.

SEVEN

Next morning, Dorus called on
one of the city judges and told
him his story. Workmen were sent
to dig at the spot where the ghost
had disappeared.

Soon their spades struck metal.
Dorus watched as they scraped away
the soil and uncovered rusty chains.

Dorus knelt down and cleaned
away the soil with his hands. Inside
the chains were bones – the bones
of a man. It was clear he had been
murdered, wrapped in chains, and
hidden here.

Dorus turned to the judge. "Killers wrap their victims in chains to stop the spirit rising and haunting them. But some ghosts are strong enough to escape. This is why the spirit wanders the earth at night. It needs a proper grave."

The workmen took off the chains and laid the bones carefully in a cloth. The judge gave orders for them to be buried properly.

At last the poor, tortured spirit was laid to rest.

The ghost found peace in its grave. Dorus found peace in his house, for the spirit in chains never returned.

Pertinax looked around Pliny's
fine garden. In its centre stood a
young tree.

"Is that the spot?" he whispered.

Pliny rose to his feet. "This story
happened in Athens, we agreed,"
he smiled.

But the boy couldn't tear his eyes from the tree. He could picture the ancient ghost wailing and rattling its chains. A bright-eyed parrot stared at him from the branches. "Poor parrot," he sighed.

Pliny wrapped an arm around the boy's shoulder and shook him gently. "The gods are kind, Pertinax. We all find rest in the end."

"Not if you're a bird," the boy replied and went back into the kitchen.

"Ah, there you are, Pertinax," Augusta smiled. She was stitching wings onto a boiled hare to make it look like a flying creature. "Have a slice of roast parrot!"

The boy shook his head. "No thanks, Grandma, I'm not hungry."

With his work done, Pertinax prepared to leave, as Pliny and his guests were starting their feast.

Before he went, he stood by the door and listened.

"Ah!" the guests cried over and over again. "Such fine food, Pliny. You give the best feasts in Rome!"

"I have the best cook," said Pliny.

"That is true!" a grand lady sighed. "If only my cook could make parrot heads as fine as yours!"

Pertinax smiled and ran home happily through the dusty streets.

But that night, the boy didn't sleep. He couldn't. The sound of rattling chains was keeping him awake...

AFTERWORD

Pliny was a Roman lawyer who lived from AD 63–113. He wrote lots of letters to Roman emperors, friends and people he worked with. The letters can still be read today.

Historians learned a lot about Roman life from the letters of Pliny. They told of the famous day when the Mount Vesuvius volcano erupted and swallowed the city of Pompeii. Pliny's uncle was one of the people who died there.

Pliny also wrote about some of the fantastic feasts the rich people in Rome would eat. All the food in this story was eaten at some time in Rome – even parrot heads and pheasant tongues, hares with wings and roast boar filled with singing birds.

One of Pliny's most famous letters contains the story about the ghost in the garden. He told it just as it's told here. It's one of the world's first-ever ghost stories.

Is it true? We will never know. But Pliny was a clever man, and he believed it. The Romans believed some odd things. We can be sure most Romans would have believed Pliny's famous ghost story. Do you?

ROME, 387 BC

The cruel Gauls are attacking Rome.
High on the Capitol Hill, the priests have been
defending the temple of Juno for weeks. But food
is running out and their only hope of help is from
the army of Lord Furius. Will he arrive in time?
And what will they do if he doesn't?

Roman Tales are exciting, funny stories based
on historical events - short chapters and
illustrations throughout are perfect for
building reading confidence.

ISBN 978 0 7136 8963 1   £4.99

ROME, AD 51

Deri is in prison. The outspoken Celt was
heard criticising Rome and now faces execution
in the morning. Luckily, his cell mate Caratacus is
a very special prisoner indeed – a British chief.
He believes there is a way to save both their
skins, but first he will need Deri's help.

Roman Tales are exciting, funny stories based
on historical events – short chapters and
illustrations throughout are perfect for
building reading confidence.

ISBN 978 0 7136 8960 0   **£4.99**

ROME, AD 64

Rome is a dangerous place. Especially on the
day of the chariot races, and for a young girl.
When Mary finds herself the only witness to
a terrible crime, soon it is not just the thieves
and drunks that she has to worry about, but
someone far more cruel and powerful...

Roman Tales are exciting, funny stories based
on historical events - short chapters and
illustrations throughout are perfect for
building reading confidence.

ISBN 978 0 7136 8970 9   £4.99